For Anne and Lee, who, like Dickens himself,
have a gift for bringing stories to life. —D.H.

For my children, Jack and Annie—remember that stories matter. With gratitude to
C.S., J.R.R., and J.K.,
my favorite British storytellers. —J.H.

•

Text copyright © 2012 by Deborah Hopkinson
Illustrations copyright © 2012 by John Hendrix

Visit us on the Web! www.randomhouse.com/kids
Educators and librarians, for a variety of teaching tools, visit us at www.randomhouse.com/teachers

Library of Congress Cataloging-in-Publication Data
Hopkinson, Deborah.
A boy called Dickens / Deborah Hopkinson ; illustrations by John Hendrix.—1st ed.
p. cm.
Summary: Narrates the tale of twelve-year-old Charles Dickens who, despite poverty and long hours of factory work,
still has time to discover and share the stories of other residents of 1824 London.
Includes author's note about Dickens' life and some of the books he wrote.
ISBN 978-0-375-86732-3 (trade) — ISBN 978-0-375-96732-0 (glb) — ISBN 978-0-375-98740-3 (ebook)
1. Dickens, Charles, 1812–1870—Juvenile fiction. [1. Dickens, Charles, 1812–1870—Fiction. 2. Authors—Fiction.
3. London (England)—History—19th century—Fiction. 4. Great Britain—History—Victoria, 1837–1901—Fiction.]
I. Hendrix, John, ill. II. Title.
PZ7.H778125Boy 2012
[Fic]—dc22
2010048531

The text of this book is set in Clarendon.
The illustrations were rendered in graphite, pen-and-ink, and fluid acrylics.
Book design by Rachael Cole

MANUFACTURED IN MALAYSIA
10 9 8 7 6 5 4 3 2 1
First Edition

A BOY CALLED

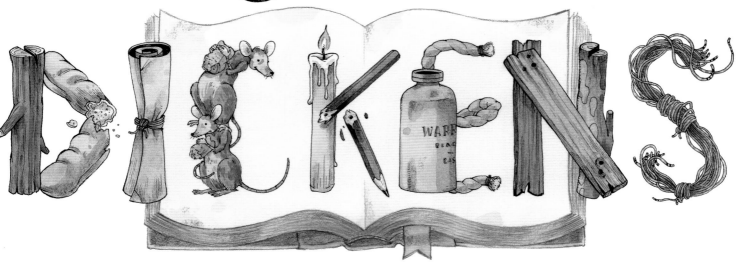

DICKENS

WRITTEN BY

DEBORAH HOPKINSON

ILLUSTRATED BY

JOHN HENDRIX

schwartz & wade books · new york

THIS IS OLD LONDON,

on a winter morning long ago. Come along, now.
We are here to search for a boy called Dickens.

He won't be easy to find. The fog has crept in,
silent as a ghost, to fold the city in cold, gray arms.

Maybe the boy is down by the river—the thick,
black Thames. There are ragged children here, to be
sure, scrambling for bits of copper and wood to sell.

Or maybe he's dashing into that schoolroom along with the other lads, their cheeks pink from the cold and crumbs of hot buns still on their lips.

Oh, look! There he is—that skinny twelve-year-old, huddled in a doorway, wearing a worn, patched jacket. He is watching the schoolboys with hungry eyes. But though he'd like something to eat, he longs for their books even more. Almost all of his own books, which he loved so well, were lugged to the pawnshop long ago.

Suddenly Dickens is gone. Hurry! Let's not lose him in the twisting, turning alleys.

There he is, running to that run-down, rickety house by the river. Are we brave enough to follow him?

The boy steps inside and coughs in the bitter
cold. He tries not to hear the squeaking of the rats
that live in the rafters. This is Warren's, a blacking
factory, which makes polish for gentlemen's boots.

Dickens ties on a ragged apron and climbs onto his stool. Before him is a table crowded with little pots of polish, sheets of paper, string, scissors, and a paste pot. This is what he does:

He covers one pot of polish with a piece of oilpaper. He adds a piece of blue paper. He cuts some string to tie the papers snugly around the top.

He clips everything close and neat. He dabs paste on the back of a label and sticks it on. Done.

Then he starts all over again with the next, and the next, and the next, and the next.

After a bit, a scruffy lad named Bob Fagin speaks up. "Will you tell a story today, Dickens? I laughed so hard at your tale yesterday, my ribs still hurt."

Dickens shrugs, then says, "Well, something odd did happen as I tramped through the fog this morning."

Bob Fagin leans close. "Do tell!"

And so Dickens begins:

"Just as I came down Hungerford Stairs, a boy slammed into me so hard we both fell. He jumped up and looked around wildly.

"'Are you a thief?' I asked.

"'No!' he cried. 'My stepfather put me to work at Murdstone's warehouse. But I couldn't bear it another minute. I'm running away.'"

"But where could he go?" asks Bob Fagin.

"I wondered that very thing," says Dickens, his eyes alight. "It seems that the boy—he said his name was David—was heading to Dover, near the sea. He hoped to throw himself on the mercy of an aunt he'd never set eyes on. Aunt Betsey, he called her."

Bob Fagin whispers, "Go on. What happened next?"

Before Dickens can answer, the door flies open and the foreman strides in.

"Silence!" he commands. "Back to work."

We must wait a long time for the
workday to be done—ten hours.
Finally, Dickens and the other boys
spill out into the darkness.

Dickens shoves his hands into his pockets to keep them warm. He starts home through the crowded streets, passing vendors who bellow,

ONLY a HA'PENNY

HOT BAKED POTATOES

CHESTNUTS HERE!

He stops to buy his meal—a penny loaf of bread, a small hunk of cheese—and splurges on a four-penny plate of beef from a cookshop.

Then Dickens walks on, surrounded by
pickpockets; ladies with shattered hopes;
a miserly old man; a young gentleman with
great expectations; a proud, heartless girl.
There are lawyers, clerks, convicts, and
keepers of old curiosity shops.

There are even ghosts and spirits. And
children like Dickens, trying to hold on to
a dream.

All these characters and their stories swirl about the boy like the fog. They follow him to a dingy house, where he climbs a narrow staircase to a tiny attic room. Inside are his cot, a washbasin, and the shelf to hold half of his loaf of bread for morning.

Dickens carefully lights a candle and reaches under the thin blanket for his most prized possessions—a pencil and slate. For the first time, he smiles.

Soon his drab room disappears. All day long, the story of the runaway boy called David has filled his thoughts. Now he begins to scratch out David's journey—as the runaway trudges day after day, stopping to sell his jacket for a few pennies to buy some bread, reaching his aunt's house at last.

Dickens stops writing and closes his eyes, picturing the scene in his mind.

Aunt Betsey is in her garden when she spies David.

"Get along! No boys here!"

"If you please, aunt, I am your nephew," he replies, surprising her so much that she sits down flat on the garden path.

Dickens tries to imagine what David will say to convince his aunt to take him in. But by now his eyes are heavy with sleep. He blows out the candle and pulls his thin blanket close. He is all alone.

Is the boy called Dickens an orphan like the runaway boy in his imaginary tale? Reader, he is not. Where, then, is his family? That mystery must wait for morning.

When Dickens wakes, it is Sunday. He will not go to church, but instead makes his way to Marshalsea Prison.

Yes, prison. Here, huddled in a room, are his mother and father, sister Letitia, and little brothers Frederick and Alfred.

Mr. Dickens has been put into debtors' prison for not paying his forty-pound debt to the baker. Since his wife and younger children have nowhere else to go, they live here too.

"Take a warning from your poor, pitiful father, Charles,"
Mr. Dickens tells his son as he stirs the fire. "If a man is paid
twenty pounds a year, and spends nineteen pounds, nineteen
shillings, and sixpence, he will be happy. But even one more
shilling spent will make him as wretched as me."

Young Dickens looks into the fire. He misses the old days,
when they all lived together. He misses his books and school.
If things go on like this, he will lose hope of growing up to
be someone—maybe even a writer.

WINTER GIVES WAY

to the pale light of spring. And one May morning, the Dickens family, bags and bundles in hand, walk away from prison at last.

Mr. Dickens has settled his debt. A friend will take them in. An inheritance is on the horizon. In other words, something has turned up. The family is saved.

But has the boy been saved?

By now the family can get by without the six shillings he brings home. But though he has devoured books the way most boys eat candy; though he can tell tales that hold listeners spellbound, and even write little stories of his own, Charles is still sent off to work ten hours a day, six days a week.

What careless parents to neglect their boy this way!

Then one day his father visits the factory. He sees
Charles on his stool, working, fast, fast, fast—so fast that
people outside stop and watch through the window.

At last Mr. Dickens opens his eyes. Most likely his own
pride is hurt—he is ashamed to see his son on display.

We cannot hear exactly what is said, but Mr. Dickens quarrels with the factory owner.

Charles is sent home.

His mother—and Charles never can forgive her for this—tries to patch up the quarrel so that he can return to work.

But his father, thank goodness, says no.

Now, once again, let us follow the boy.
It's a clear, sunny morning. He is walking
briskly; his eyes are bright. And what's that
he's carrying?

Yes, a book. Today Dickens is going to
Camden Town, to school. At last!

There are piles of books here, and boys full of fun. There are also mice. The schoolboys love to keep white mice as pets—in desks, in drawers, and even in hatboxes.

Charles doesn't mind the mice.

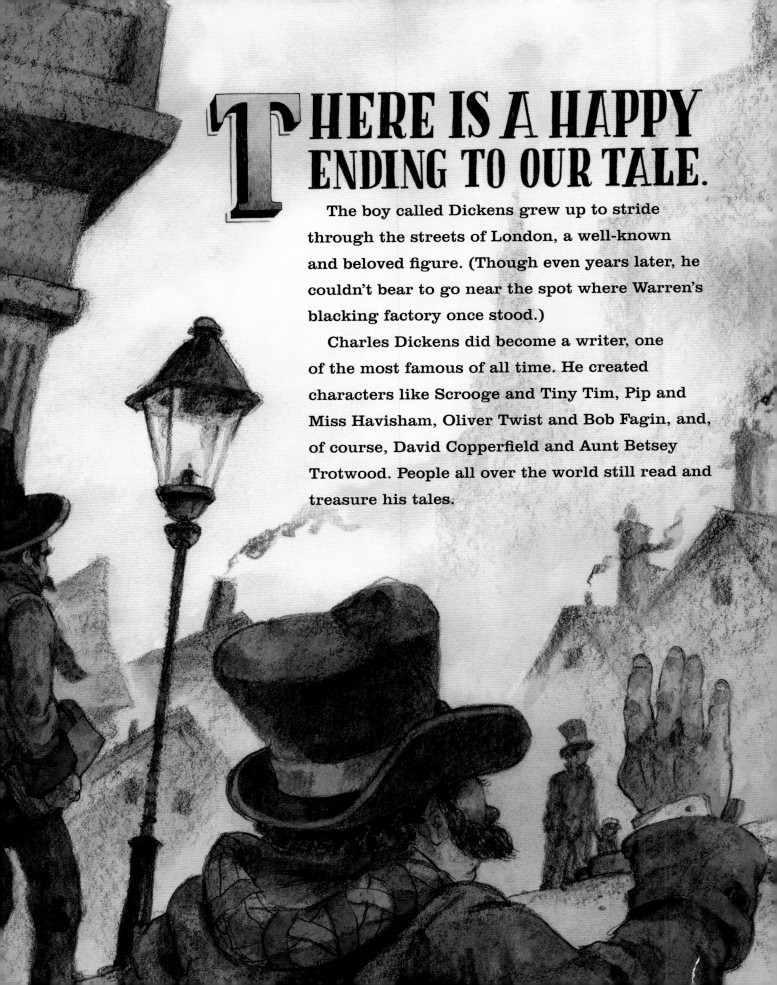

THERE IS A HAPPY ENDING TO OUR TALE.

The boy called Dickens grew up to stride through the streets of London, a well-known and beloved figure. (Though even years later, he couldn't bear to go near the spot where Warren's blacking factory once stood.)

Charles Dickens did become a writer, one of the most famous of all time. He created characters like Scrooge and Tiny Tim, Pip and Miss Havisham, Oliver Twist and Bob Fagin, and, of course, David Copperfield and Aunt Betsey Trotwood. People all over the world still read and treasure his tales.

For years Dickens kept the story of his own
childhood a secret. Yet it is a story worth telling.
For it helps us remember how much we all might
lose when a child's dreams don't come true.

A NOTE ABOUT THIS STORY

A Boy Called Dickens is based on incidents in the life of the novelist Charles Dickens (1812 to 1870). Dickens was born in Portsmouth, England, one of eight children. (Two had died before this story takes place, and the youngest had not yet been born.)

Charles Dickens loved books and reading, and in Portsmouth, his parents could afford to send him to school. But when Dickens was ten, the family moved to London and began to struggle financially. Shortly after his twelfth birthday, when this story takes place, he was sent to work in a factory. Dickens kept this period of his life a secret for many years. It wasn't until 1847 that he wrote about this time in an autobiographical piece that he shared with his friend and biographer John Forster.

Dickens never published a full account of his life, but we can see traces of his childhood in many of his works, especially *David Copperfield*. Like Dickens, young David is neglected and sent to work in a factory; David also visits Marshalsea Prison, where the novelist's father was jailed. Eventually David escapes his factory life and is taken in by his aunt, Betsey Trotwood.

Besides playing a part in his novels, Dickens's boyhood experiences helped to shape his interest in social reform. He wrote articles about child neglect and gave money to hospitals and charities for the poor.

While much of *A Boy Called Dickens* is drawn closely from the fragments about his life that Dickens wrote, this story is fiction. I added dialogue and imagined the part where Dickens begins writing *David Copperfield*. (Dickens really did work with a boy named Bob Fagin, though. You might recognize Fagin as a character in *Oliver Twist*.)

Writing this story was a special pleasure, as Dickens has been one of my favorite authors since I was a girl. Every Christmas Eve, I stay up late reading *A Christmas Carol*. I hope you get as lost in Dickens's world as I do.

—Deborah Hopkinson